Laurence Housman

**All-fellows**

Seven legends of lower redemption with insets in verse

Laurence Housman

**All-fellows**
*Seven legends of lower redemption with insets in verse*

ISBN/EAN: 9783337150181

Printed in Europe, USA, Canada, Australia, Japan

Cover: Foto ©Andreas Hilbeck / pixelio.de

More available books at **www.hansebooks.com**

# ALL-FELLOWS
## SEVEN LEGENDS OF LOWER REDEMPTION WITH INSETS IN VERSE BY LAURENCE HOUSMAN

LONDON: KEGAN PAUL, TRENCH,
TRÜBNER AND CO., LIMITED, PATER-
NOSTER HOUSE, CHARING CROSS ROAD
1896

# PREFACE

AYBE some word of explanation is owing in regard to the sequence of verse which accompanies and divides these stories. Being only a portion of a projected whole, it does not go more than half-way to the final realisation of its scheme, and remains so far the statement of an essentially incomplete phase of spiritual emotion. Unless thus reckoned with, expressions which were meant to be relative or conditional rather than positive, dramatic rather than theoretic, will cause a shock to

## Preface

readers who imagine that an assault is meant on things which they hold sacred.

It is clear that if one endeavours to give in dramatic form the struggling of Jacob with his Angel, strange words have to be put into his mouth. Unfortunately there are to be found, to sit in judgment, minds of a literal persuasion, that take from the artist his own soul, to set it in the image that he has made.

# CONTENTS

# CONTENTS

Never shall life clear utterance show
  To reach the hearts of men :
Hark back three thousand years, and know
  How tongues had labour then,

When God, who gathers north and south,
  To marvel at His ways,
Opened of old the ass's mouth,
  And filled it with His praise.

But when Love bowed His Body whole
  To death, for the dark East,
Then hung before men's eyes a Soul
  More dumb than any beast.

1                              A

His Lips, who spake as no man spake,
   Nothing at all availed ;
They gave Him vinegar to take,
   And wagged their heads and railed.

So ye the seers, and ye that seek,
   Fellows with Him must be :
Only the dumb of heart can speak,
   And the blind think they see.

If all the needs in all the hearts
   Of all the world were one,
We could afford to drop our parts,
   Nor wait to watch the sun,

To count the days that gather in
   Toward the wished-for end,
Where pleasure can no more be sin,
   Nor friend want help of friend.

But now how fast the coil of things
   Holds each man to his part,
While here, with hidden wants, there clings
   To each an alien heart !

Nor by myself can I be freed
   To lay me down and die,
Because of all the hearts in need
   Of comfort less than I !

THOU breast of all bright things, thou Earth,
   Where I was lapped ere day
Drew me from darkness unto birth,
   Fair mother of my clay,

Now night and day, where'er I go,
   I seem to hear thee cry,
" O child, what hast thou learned to know
   "Of signs beneath the sky ? "

And I bend down, and answer back,
  " I learn there is no rest
" On sea or land for those who lack
  " The covering of thy breast."


Then she : " What hast thou there, weak
      heart,
  " That will not set thee free ? "
" Dear grief, from which I cannot part,
  " And love, too strong for me !


" And better to my heart than rest
  " This love that burns like fire ;
" And dearer than your breast the breast
  " Of grief that quells desire ! "

# THE LOVELY MESSENGERS

—

# THE LOVELY MESSENGERS

T was Christmas Eve, and the door of the farm was shut to keep out the cold. A woman crept into the porch, and knocked timidly, then for a while waited.

While waiting, she leaned face and hands against one of the side-posts ; and from head to foot a slow trembling took hold of her, of cold, and fear, and weakness.

After the third knock a bar was let down from within, and the door swung wide on its hinges ; warm light streamed out, showing the figure of the supplicant. " Let me in, or I shall die ! " the poor thing said, with a heavy forward leaning.

" Who are you ? " asked the farm-woman,

7

who had the door in her hand. "Ah, it's *you!*" There was recognition in the tone but not welcome.

"Who is it?" called out the farmer from the ingle-corner. "Don't keep the door a-gape, letting in all the cold!"

"'Tis Molly, the bad wench," answered the woman; "and she's big; to her shame be it said. Her time is not far off!"

"I won't have her here!" cried the farmer. "Let her carry her shame away from honest folks' doors! Shut it—you there, I say!"

The door was shut-to again, and barred. Molly turned and crept meekly away through the barton, past the cow-pens and out-houses. Presently she stopped, with deep shudderings from head to foot, and leaned against a stack of hurdles for support.

"I can't go on!" she whispered. "I shall die!"

Within wooden walls she heard a rustle of straw, and the snored breathings of live-stock.

"I shall die, I shall die!" she moaned.

# The Lovely Messengers

Her hand fell on a wooden bolt, shot home loosely into its socket : at a weak push it yielded, and the door creaked inwards. She entered to a warm vapourish atmosphere of animals and fermenting litter. In a corner where the straw seemed freshest and cleanest she lay down, and felt comparative peace for a while take hold of her wrenched body.

Close by went a slow munching, where the steer and the ass's colt stood loosely stalled side by side. As they munched the extra portion given them for that night's meal, they talked together of the Feast which Heaven and Earth were even then beginning to hold.

" This is the night of our inheritance," said the steer ; " our fathers have told us, as their fathers told them ; so it has come down to us through all the generations till to-day. I feel as if I had been there myself, and seen the Holy One who came to save the souls of those that do daily beat and ill-use us."

" Tell me," said the ass's colt, " for I am young ! What were They like, the Mother and her Babe ? "

The steer said: "She wore a white wimple, with a crown on it, and a blue robe with the Magnificat broidered about its border. And He had a golden orb in His right hand, and a light round His head; and as soon as He was born He spoke to her."

"What did He say?" asked the colt.

"He said, 'Hail Mary, the Lord is with thee!' And at that the father of my fathers, and the father of your fathers bent their knees, and began worshipping Him. And ever since then, once a year, our hearts are opened, so that we know how to worship Him and do Him meet service. But not in this world shall we learn to serve Him daily, as men do; and not for many worlds to serve him continually, as the angels do."

"When men have become as angels," said the colt, "perhaps we shall be in the place of men. How good it will be, then, to serve Him daily!"

"Good indeed!" replied the steer. "Kneel down; we are near the hour of the blissful Birth."

## The Lovely Messengers

Said the colt : "Was there no trouble at that Birth?"

"I do not know," answered the steer ; "but the meek Mother did not cry, nor the Babe, when It was born, wail."

Presently, while the beasts bent worshipping there, a shuddering cry came from the straw ; again and again it was repeated, and the beasts knew and recognised the great central note of nature since the Fall, the cry of a mother in her pains. By-and-bye was added to it the cry of a human when it first draws breath. Feeble and weak, Molly stretched out her arms, and caught and laid the naked life in her breast.

The steer and the ass's colt looked on with mild and reverent fear. "The Holy Child and His Mother," said they, "have sent us these to watch and guard for a remembrance of Them."

They heard the mother moan, "Bring water, and a priest, lest my child die in sin, and be not baptized into Christ!" And as midnight grew near, they heard her say again,

" It dies, it dies ! Oh, for a priest, and a drop of water ! "

Then for the love of Christ, on this night of His birth, the steer and the ass's colt rose up to do Him service. They went out softly by the door that lay ajar, and stole down side by side to the church that shone lighted below the hill.

All the way, over their heads, shone the Northern Lights with flicker and throb : and they knew that there, out of gold harp-strings like corn, angels were reaping melodies to God. When they got to the church it was the time of the midnight Mass. Looking in through a window they saw the Crib, and all the congregation kneeling before it. Our Lady had on a white wimple, with a gold crown on it, and a blue robe ; and the Holy Child held an orb, and wore a halo round His head.

Then the two beasts beat softly upon the door with their fore-feet ; and the steer lowed, and the ass brayed for the priest to come out and carry Christ to the child's soul.

# The Lovely Messengers

One of the servers came out to drive them away ; but they bore all his strokes patiently, and stayed there waiting for the priest to come forth. "Let us wait quietly !" said the steer at last. "When the Mass is over he will come."

So silently they watched, and heard the Sanctus sung, and bowed themselves at sacring-bell ; till presently the congregation came out, and last of all the priest.

The priest was in a hurry to get back to his bed and be warm ; and lo, and behold, down knelt the ass right in the way before his feet ! Whichever way he turned, there the steer and the ass hemmed him in.

Soon the priest began thinking, what marvel was this ? Had the two beasts that worshipped at Christ's cradle been sent by God, in reward to him for his services, to bear him home ? "Non dignus sum !" said he, crossing himself ; and therewith he sat himself on the back of the beast, and rode.

Ass and steer walked on together ; but when they came to the dividing of the ways that led to the priest's house, and to the farm, by no means could the priest get himself brought nearer where he would be. There in the cross roads the colt danced him round like a wind-worshipping weather-cock.

At length, so stirred was he with resentment at the brute so ill-fulfilling the heavenly dictates of its mission, that lifting up his staff he struck the colt roundly three times, bidding it go on in the name of the Blessed Trinity.

And thereat his eyes were opened, and he saw One leading the ass in the way up to the farm. And she had on a blue robe, and a white wimple with a crown over it, and a Child on her arm bearing an orb; and light rayed round them.

Then the priest was so stricken with fear, that he tried with all his courage to fall off the colt, but could not; and presently at the crest of the hill they turned in by the farm-yard gate. Then the ass stood still, and the priest found his feet trembling on firm ground.

Over the heavens shot the Northern Lights, wherein were the angels making melodies to

## The Lovely Messengers

God; but within the stable was more light than came from them. Looking in, he saw that the ass and the steer had entered, and were bowed forward upon their knees ; and between them was she of the blue robe and wimple and crown, bearing a Babe.

The priest fell face forward to the earth ; and when he lifted himself there was no light within the stable save that which came from the Northern Lights : and he entering saw a young mother lying asleep, with a new-born babe in her arms.

But around and over her poor clothing lay the white wimple, and the blue robe broidered with the words of the Magnificat : the same which he had seen worn by Her who went before, leading the ass, and bearing the Blessed Child.

Long through the night the new-born lamb
    Utters its first complaint ;
By the cold body of its dam
    The cry goes low and faint.


Till faint against the dawn the birth
    Which bears a twilight's span
Shall pass, and let alone to earth
    The sorry needs of man.


Now, ere the covering darkness yields,
    Lie down, dear lamb, lie down :
Better to die here in the fields
    Than yonder in the town ;

16

Where fast before the butchering knife
  A dumb death thins the herd.
O, better now to part from life
  While life seems worth a word !

Out on the downs the shepherds cry,
  The silly sheep-dogs yelp.
Then, quickly ease my heart and die,
  Lest I should bring you help !

LIVING, I feel the feet that tread
  My burial-plot of ground,
As if they grudged the tired dead
  A sleep that is too sound.

Tread softly, you, and you ; for I—
  Truly I know you not !
Leave, where the dead man has to lie,
  The quiet of his lot.

17                               B

But if, at crossing of love's ways,
   Feet from a distant land
Stood now, where after many days
   I shall come, not to stand :

Then there would grow a light above
   This darkness of my breast,
And I should know the feet I love
   Had touched my place of rest.

# THE TRUCE OF GOD

# THE TRUCE OF GOD

MONG the beasts of the forest word went that a holy man was come to live in their midst : at the base of a rock, which would give him shelter from the noonday's heat, he had wattled himself a shed. Out of the undergrowth the animals watched him by day, and saw him digging himself a well, or searching the earth for roots ; and at night, when he slept, they came through the door of his shed, and snuffed at him where he lay. Then they said : " He is at peace with us, for there is no smell of blood on him. Let him be ! " And after the herds and the timid kinds, that love to be at peace with man, came the lion and the other beasts of prey ; and they looked and said : " He is no hunter, but a lover of peace." Therefore they let him be.

Soon the hermit, looking quietly out from his hut, saw that none of the beasts had any fear of him at all ; but that to each kind he was become as one of themselves. Their eyes put off the startled look that comes at the sight of man ; and, instead of dread, the hermit began to read in them the joys and sorrows that underlay all the life of the forest. In a little while the furry passers-by came not only to know him by sight, but to be friends.

When the heat of the sun lay heavy upon the forest, and all the air was like a furnace in the sick drought of noon, then the shadow under the rock by the wattled hut was the coolest place to lie in : and the hinds would come with their young ones, and the black wild boars, and the little coneys, and all lie quietly together round the hermit as he prayed. There, too, a buck that was lame, and could not get down to the drinking-place, came and begged water out of the hermit's

22

well ; and always whatever he met looked him in the eyes, and was friendly.

The beasts that fought together at pairing time came to him with their wounds ; and mothers brought their sick young, and laid them at his feet. And the hermit found that to him God had given healing power over all the life in the forest. His peaceful feet, whose sound all the animals knew too well to fear, led him to sights that are not given to other men : he saw fierce beasts gentle at their wooing, and jackals tender over their young ; and the more he saw, the more he loved God and all the orders that He had made.

Yet not only on joy did his heart grow wise, but on sorrow. Hinds came and wept to him for their bucks killed at the drinking-place by the beasts of blood : and he beheld how famine and sudden ravages of disease swept over the forest and struck down the herds in scores. And disease, indeed, his healing touch could help to drive away, but not famine. Yet God ever granted much to his prayers.

# All-Fellows

Once, at the time when the young deer were yet helpless and dependent upon their mothers for food, a hind fell from the edge of the rock under which the hermit had built his hut, and had her neck broken in the fall. Her little ones, who had been following her where she went, crept down, and found her dead body lying, and cried pitifully, knowing that now they must die also, being without food. Then the hermit gathered them in his arms, and prayed to God for them that their lives might be spared. All night he prayed; and about dawn the hind lifted her head and bleated the feeding-call to her young.

But not long afterwards, when her little ones were strong and able to go alone, the hind came back to the hermit, and lay down with her head between his knees, and so died.

Now after the hermit had lived many years in the forest, there came to him one day a lion carrying a young child in its mouth. And the child, for all that the brute held him in its teeth, was not wounded or afraid. The hermit, being sure that what came in such strange wise must have been sent to him by God's will, took the child to be to him as his own son. Out of the forest he called a hind to suckle it; and the child throve and grew.

Soon, when its limbs were grown big and strong, the child began to learn from the hermit all the gentle parts of speech that were needed between them in that lonely place : and, as time went on, the love between them was wonderful. The hermit taught him of peace and salvation, and of the love of God ; but the child looked at the stars and the trees, and listened to the wind and the cries of beasts: nothing else did he seem to understand. He went and played with the young roes and hinds, and crept into the dark lairs of beasts ; and, for love of the hermit, nothing in all the forest would do him harm.

Living the wild open life, the boy grew in strength; but more and more the restlessness of unknown desires took hold of him. He stretched out his big limbs, and sighed because he was so strong ; and then he would go to his foster-father, and ask about the earth and the ways of men, and hear only of the love of God, and of gentleness and peace.

One day he put his arm round the neck of his foster-hind, and went down with her to the drinking-place; and just as they were coming there with the rest of the deer, that part of the herd which was before them turned and fled, as there fell by the water's edge a young buck pulled down by some beast of prey.

When the boy went back, and asked his father the meaning of the blood and the hind's terror, the hermit told him that it was but nature, and as God willed, who had made each animal to live after its own kind. Again the youth looked at himself with his great growth of arms, and sighed. After that, whenever his foster-mother went down to drink, he went also, putting his arm across her like a yoke, for he knew that nothing in the forest would do harm to him. And presently, partly in malice, but partly in tenderness of heart, one by one he brought all the roes and hinds down with him to drink, covering them with

26

the shelter of his arm that they might not be hurt.

In a little while the lions were half-famished, and complaining for lack of food ; and the hermit began to have knowledge of his son's ways with the hinds down at the drinking-place. He said to the youth : " My son, you do not well : you must leave all the beasts to go their own way, as God has made it good for them ! Doubt not that nothing falls without it be His will."

Then the youth went no more with the hinds to the drinking-place ; but he sighed, looking at his long arms, and stretching them out : for he came of a hunter's breed.

Now time went on, and he grew near to being a man ; and more and more his foster-father loved him as the apple of his own eye, yet little could he teach him of the love of God. And the youth roamed far and wide through the forest, restless with strength and the fire of manhood, yet finding no use for the quick coursings of his blood.

One day, as he strayed into far off parts

that bordered the ways of men, he came upon a party of hunters, and, watching them, saw the bow drawn, and heard the arrow sing to its prey. Then he laughed loud at that, finding the nature which from his birth God had given him. A month later he came back to his father's hut with the prowess and the spoils of a hunter.

Then there was fear through all that part of the forest, where no hunter had ever yet come ; for the youth had brought with him the smell of blood shed by man. The hermit was shaken by doubt, and troubled with a divided mind.

"Lay down, my son," he said, "your arrows and your bow ; for you bring tribulation instead of peace to the place that has reared you ! "

"Nay, father," answered the youth, "for this is the nature which God has given me. Give me leave, therefore, to go hence, and now and again I will return to you, when the home-feeling grows on me ; but here I will not trouble you."

# The Truce of God

So the hermit let him go, and the youth promised that when a day came he would return. On his forth-going he went down toward the drinking-place, and there he saw coming along the track the hind that had been his foster-mother, and whom he still loved. But when she saw him she sprang away startled down to the water, because of the smell of blood that was on him ; and there, just when she reached the pool's edge, out sprang a lion, and with his paw struck her across the spine so that it was broken, and she fell dead without a cry. But the great brute scenting danger sprang back into cover of the forest, and the youth's arrow sang after him at a venture, striking him behind the loin and wounding him sorely.

To the hermit's cell early on the morrow came the lion dragging a lamed limb, with an arrow sticking in the wound, and the hermit drew out the arrow, and with his weeping salved the wound and healed it, making the limb whole and strong. But the days of his peace were over : love for his son, and love

for the lower kinds could not strive in his
heart, so fast the love of his son came upper-
most. And no thought could he have of
blame for him : "Seeing," he said, "that it
is the nature God has given him, therefore I
should do wrong to bind him."

So between himself and the beasts there
began to be shadows of doubt, and they came
to him no more without fear or hindrance,
but stood at a distance, seeming to say with
timid eyes, "Is the son you love, who sheds
our blood, with you, or are you alone?" And
ever more and more, as time went on, his
heart yearned toward the absent youth, who
was dearer to him than his own life, and who
yet did not return.

Till it happened one day again, as before,
that the lion came, dragging its body, and
grievously maimed, to be healed by the hermit's hands. Then at the sight his heart
leapt, for he said within himself, "My son is
here again, very soon I shall see him!"
Therefore gladly and in pity he healed the
beast of its wound.

# The Truce of God

But when all was done, and the limb made whole, lo, the beast bowed down and licked his feet, weeping as never beast wept before, and could make no end of showing thanks and sorrow, until, with his blessing, it turned about and went.

Then, it being the heat of the day, the hermit lay down and slept till evening ; and when he woke, there at his feet the lion crouched, watching him, and weeping. And when it saw his eyes open, it turned and sprang away into the forest.

The hermit rose, and looked out, and there at his feet in the twilight lay the body of his son, dead, with his bow yet in his hand, and his arrows in their sheath. Looking, he saw the marks of claws and of teeth, and knew by what death his son had been taken from him. And at that knowledge all his mild heart became charged with grief and passion and rage, and the lust for revenge made him mad.

He stooped and kissed the dead lips ; and out of the hand he took the bow, and the sheath full of arrows, and he went down to

the drinking-place and waited there, that he
might have vengeance of his son's death.
"Nay," he cried in his heart, "for I did evil
and not good, in that I healed twice the beast
of blood that my son would have slain."

He waited till past midnight ; and one by
one all the forest kinds had come down and
drunk of the water ; but still his enemy had
not come.

Presently, in the solitude and silence, he
heard the sound of a beast coming down to
the water to drink ; then he made ready an
arrow, and pointed it toward the track.

Down the way from under the trees came
the great lion of the forest ; and by his side
walked the hermit's son, with his arm thrown
over the beast's neck like a yoke. All his
body shone with a soft light, and thereon
were the wounds left by the lion's teeth and
claws ; and he went down, carrying his bow
and arrows, like a mighty hunter before the
Lord.

The hermit saw how the two went down
into the water together ; but when, having

drunk, the beast turned and sprang up the bank, the vision was gone.

Then the hermit let fall both bow and arrows, and went back eased of all grief, and kissed his son's face where he lay dead before the door of the little hut ; and there he buried him deep down, in the fear and love of God, knowing that above all fear the love of God endured. And on the morrow, all the animals that went that way came near for him to lay his hands upon their heads in blessing, and to call them his friends.

O, SAFELY in my dreams you laid,
　　Fair pardon on my heart,
And full amends to you I made
　　While we stood far apart.

But, now the far becomes the near,
　　And once again we meet,
Sorrow so holds my heart, my dear,
　　You may not hear it beat.

A day ago, an hour, and how
　　I longed to find you near ;
Now round me grow your arms, and now
　　My heart has died for fear !

34

And ghastlier thought takes shape behind,
  Lest, if I love you more,
I, some dark morning, wake to find
  You dead against my door !

🐦

With me early, with me late,
  The face of my spent youth :
Of youth that made a friend of fate,
  And thought the friendship truth.

But now 'tis—how to bear the sun !
  When fate demands, o'er all
The ills I wish to do, the one
  I struggle to let fall.

With me early, with me late,
  A bitter thing to rue :
The wrong set down for me by fate,
  The wrong I would not do.

SEND forth thy winds, O God, to blow
  The fever from my brain ;
Let all Thy rains and rivers flow
  To wash away my stain !

And when of all its thousand ills
  My body is set free,
Then in Thy mercy bid the hills
  Bow down and cover me.

And smother out this vital spark
  That binds me in Thy sight ;
Give darkness, that it may be dark,
  And heal my eyes of light !

# THE HEART OF THE SEA

●

 FISHERMAN came to the priest's cell, which lay rock-hewn above the chapel on the headland. ˙ " Father," said he, " come down with me, and bless my nets ; for 'twill be three days now that I have caught nothing."

" Nay, is it not more ? " replied the priest, as he rose : and, laying his hand on the fellow's arm, he could feel how want and misery had made a skeleton of the strong man.

" That was before I confessed," muttered the other. " One doesn't let that count." And together they went down the rocks seawards. From the chapel to the sea's edge went a stair cut into the steep rock, worn with the tides and slippery with weed : below lay the boat moored.

The fisherman drew the boat up to the steps, and the priest embarked ; silently they rowed off through the quiet lapping waters of the bay, under the mist of a faintly-starred night.

"Where has your fishing been the three days ?" asked the priest at last. "Among my own grounds," answered the fisherman ; "under the deep rocks. The other men will not have me now : they are saying I bring ill-luck."

After an hour's rowing, his stroke slowed over blackened waters ; for there the line might drop many fathoms and find no bottom, and all away round huge walls of rock threw down their shade. The oars ceased.

"Wait awhile, father," said the fisherman, "and watch ; there is a sign that comes." They leaned together over the side of the boat and watched.

"Three nights there has been a sign," the man went on. Under them the water was

40

very still. "Do you see there?" He pointed : the untaught eyes of the priest could see nothing. " Down below there," said the other, " are shoals and shoals ; but I let down my nets and catch nothing."

"Is that the sign?" asked the priest.

" No. They are rich grounds ; they were my father's, and his father's before him. That is not the sign : to see fish here is nothing. There it is !"

The even noise of the water was broken by three pricks of sound : one after another three bubbles came up under the gunwale of the boat, and burst—so close that had either reached down a finger they could have touched them on the surface as they broke.

" It is the same !" said the fisherman. " That only?" " And when I let down my nets I catch nothing."

" Three days ago," asked the priest, " you confessed all?" " All but a sort of fear I have," answered the other. " Father, can the soul of a babe unborn perish?"

" It is in God's hands," was the reply.

"We poor sinners can but repent, and hope God will be pitiful."

Then the priest made the sign of the Cross over the water; and said he, "On this side, let down your nets as far as they will go." The priest knelt and prayed, while hand over hand the fisherman passed out long lengths of net, till all were let down.

"Draw in!" called the priest. The other obeyed.

"Father," said he, presently, "there is something here." In came snakey skeins of net, dark and swabby from the brine; but there was not sign of tail or fin to be seen.

"Still, there is something," said the fisherman: "I feel it coming." He hauled in the last lengths; in their midst was something small that showed palely in the gloom. He reached down his hands, and took up in them a new-born man-child, naked, and cold, and wet from the salt sea.

"Ah, my God!" cried the fisherman; and his limbs shook with fright. "Take it from me, I cannot hold it!" The priest, taking it, found it stone-cold to his touch ; yet there were in it signs of life.

He drew up a little sea-water in the hollow of his hand, and speaking in haste, " Fisherman," said he, "what name shall I give to your child ? "

The fisherman crouched himself in the bottom of the boat. " No name, no name, O Lord ! " he clamoured. " Christen it and have done, and throw it back to the fishes ! "

The priest, pouring the sea-water over the babe's forehead, said, " Babe, I baptize thee, in the name of the Father, and the Son, and the Holy Ghost." And at that its voice woke in a little cry like a sea-mew's ; and the fisherman, hearing, prayed that it might be thrown back into the sea.

The priest wrapped the child in his cloak and laid it to warm against his breast. Then he said to the other, " Now, again, let down your net into the sea." The fisherman obeyed trembling ; only he said, below his breath, " Not another, O Lord, or I leap out of the boat ! "

But soon, as he began to draw up the net, he laughed to feel its weight, and to see how hundreds went hither and thither darting in its midst. He rowed back to land, rich with a single haul ; and at the chapel-rock he and the priest parted. "Father," said he then, "have pity on me, for I fear to take the child, though it be mine. All else you bid me I will do ; but if it needs must be reared, do you rear it, for in truth that is beyond me."

So the priest took the child with him to his cell, and, bringing a goat to suckle it, cared for it as tenderly as though it had been his own. And, as time went on, 'twixt love and fear, he watched how strangely it grew, and wondered of what life it was.

Terrible was its fear of the sea, and of dreams where the feared thing cannot be kept away. Yet sea-gulls came to its call, and as the child grew began to make their nests in the carved clefts of the chapel-rock looking seaward, and over the lintel of the priest's cell, so that presently from the sea the chapel-

44

rock stood out white on the dark headland, because of the birds that made it their home.

As the boy grew he went by the name the priest had given him in baptism ; even when he became a man he was "Babe" still to all that spoke of him. He was slow of speech and slow to learn ; and all the use of life for him seemed to be to sit at the priest's door by the chapel on the lonely headland, and to gaze out over all weathers through the clustering of white gulls.

All the gentleness and thoughtfulness of his nature seemed fitting him for a life of religion and seclusion ; therefore the priest trained him in the fear and knowledge of God, and in love and pity for all things that had life. And after his twentieth year he became a priest, so that when his foster-father died he might succeed him in his holy office.

Of his parentage he but just knew. "Who," he had said, "is the fisherman who rows up to the steps, and leaves fish and fruit for us, but never comes up to the door ; and if he sees me, looks at me in fear?"

" He is your father, Babe," the Priest had answered. " And who," asked Babe, "is my mother?" The Priest told him her name. "She," he said, " was lost in the sea : none saw her die." This was before Babe went away to be trained for the priesthood.

As soon as Babe was made priest he came back to the chapel-rock, for his foster-father was already becoming old and infirm : and now often could not say his daily Mass in the chapel on the headland, which was there that Masses might be said for the souls of those lost at sea.

When Babe came there and sang his first Mass, his foster-father asked him : " What was your intention in saying your Mass ?" And Babe answered : " I said it for those that live under the sea." But more than that, or his reason for that, he did not know. His foster-father said : " All the while behind us there was a sound of wings, and of sea-water without."

No long time after the old priest died and was laid in the burial-ground above the chapel, among all the drowned bodies of the men for whose souls his life had been spent in prayer. Then Babe remained alone to sing Mass in the chapel-rock below.

Fishermen who passed by, or came to kneel in the door seeing that Mass was being said, told how all within the chapel was white with the clustering of gulls ; and how from beginning to end they kept silent, nor ever lifted a wing before the time was to go. So the story began that he was a saint, and that God had shown it to the birds ; and presently people came and besought his prayers when trouble and heavy misfortune was upon them. And all reckoned that his word did good.

Only the one fisherman who feared him, feared him not less ; and came and went, never going nearer than the foot of the steps in the chapel-rock to leave offerings of bread or fish. But a time came, and his offerings had to cease ; and the other fishermen said : " The evil luck is on you again ; go up to the sea-chapel and bid the priest bless your fish-

ing : and until you get his blessing do not
work with us ! "

For a long while he waited, hoping to find
a turn in his luck come ; but at last famine
and fear drove him, and he went.

He found Babe praying before the altar ;
and he, as soon as he turned and saw who was
there, stretched out his hands crying : "I
have waited long for your coming, father ! "

The fisherman, confounded and astonished
to find himself known, "I have been an ill
father," said he ; "from the beginning I was
that ; for I was for throwing you back into
the sea when you came out of it." And to
Babe's question he laid bare all the story of
his birth out of the sea and the night under
the dark rocks. "And now again," said he,
"luck is gone from my fishing, and last night
once more came the sign."

Together without more words they went
down into the boat, and the fisherman rowed
his son through the closing night to the place
of deep water under the rocks. And as they
leaned over the boatside, and looked into the

dead calm, up came the three bubbles, and broke in three small sighs.

Then Babe, making over it the sign of the Cross, bade let down the net as far as it might go. After he had hauled some while : " There is weight here ! said the fisherman ; and all the while Babe ceased not to pray.

Up to the boatside came a white form, young, and fair, and dead : a woman clothed in strange seaweeds, and with long yellow hair going down to her feet. The fisherman, seeing her come, shrieked and wailed, and fell down babbling for fear : therefore Babe himself lifted his fair young mother's body over the boatside. For the deep-sea life to her flesh had been but as a day ; and for all the years of her bondage, she was to the eye as on the day when her lover's faithlessness had made her go there to seek death.

All the way back the fisherman sat and yammered on the farthest thwart of the boat, making circles with his eyes, while his son rowed. And at the chapel-rock, the priest only, lifting her, bore her up to the little graveyard on the headland, where lay the cast-up bodies of drowned fishing folk.

The old fisherman followed him like a babe, and watched all he did with a witless smile. And not long before dawn they two came down into the chapel ; and there, for his mother's soul, Babe began to sing Mass.

All the gulls roused up from their nests in the crannies without, and came flocking in. " Little son, little son," called the old man, see the white birds that have come here to hear you say Mass ! " But Babe heeded not, and went on.

Presently there was a soft hustling sound in the chapel, and again the old man laughed, and cried : " Little son, little son, see the blue men who have come to hear you sing Mass ! " But Babe, as if not heeding the words, went on.

" Little son, little son," cried the old man once more, " the blue men weep as they hear you sing Mass ! " But it was the time of the elevation of the Host, and without pausing the priest went on.

50

# The Heart of the Sea

Presently he came to the words of the dismissal, "Ite, missa est !" and there was a sound of withdrawn sobs, and overhead the rush of sea-mews' wings departing. "Little son, little son," cried the old man, "the blue men are gone !" His son turned and came down from the altar. All the floor was wet and salt as a rock over which the tide has ebbed down.

"Little son, little son," cried the fisherman, "you look old !"

"Father," said Babe, "now take me back in your boat to the place of deep-water under the rocks ; to the place whence I came : the place whither you would have had me return."

The old man gabbled and laughed : so soft was he of brain he had no fear now. So together they rowed to the fishing ground beneath the high rocks.

Then Babe stripped himself as a diver, and stood up shuddering in the boat. "Kiss me, father," said he ; "and when you go home ask others to cherish you in your old age. But they that live under the sea have none to cherish them, or to teach them the word of Life."

He looked fearfully down into the sea he dreaded; yet he knew that he had in him the sea-life, and that far down under the waves sea-speech would rise up to his lips—a gift that had not been given to the Apostles on the day of Pentecost.

The fisherman laughed and said : " How you talk for a new-born babe ! Rock, cradle, rock !" And he swayed the boat from side to side. Presently he was alone, and passing his hand over his eyes : " Ah, Ah !" he went on, " I said to the priest, 'Throw it overboard'! Has the priest gone too?" And he took up the oars and rowed home.

For many days the rock-chapel was empty; till, one night of wind and roaring water, up came the sea. It filled the chapel, and dashed the mews out of their crannies, and broke the cross over the altar, and made all that was there a ruin.

At dawn the waters went down ; and there lay on the floor of the chapel a fair youth,

## The Heart of the Sea

with hands and feet pierced, and crowned
with a crown of sharp coral, the image of
one crucified for the love of Him whom he
had been down to preach in the depths of
the sea.

AMID this grave-strewn, flowerless place
  A dead man prays in stone :
Worn with the weather how the face
  Looks like a mask of bone.

From praying feet to praying hands,
  Prayer will not let him go :
Still patiently his face withstands
  God's everlasting No.

For still to all the plea he gives
  God's word long since was said :
And still the foolish faith outlives
  The mercy which lies dead.

The praying stone wears down to dust,
  And every day that dies
It proffers with a piteous trust
  The prayer that God denies.



DEAR heart, when with a twofold mind
  I pray for bitter grace;
And from my pit of torment find
  Your breath upon my face,


And hear you without thought of fear
  Bid me to guard you well,
And guide your footsteps to win clear—
  When my feet walk in hell:


I wonder, how can God be glad
  To hear men praise Him so,
Who makes His piteous earth so sad
  A lot to undergo?

Or does He, too, dip Feet in fire,
  And share the thirster's thirst ;
And listen to man's great desire
  Holding a Heart to burst?

# THE MERCIFUL DROUGHT

# THE MERCIFUL DROUGHT

**D**EEP drought was on all the forest, a drought that went down to the roots of things, so that the earth's surface chipped and cracked, and lay gaping with parched lips for something to drink. Whenever the least leaf stirred it gave out a crisp sound like fire, so dry was it become ; and every twig and branch as it moved ticked and crackled with the heat. The foot-dints of the herds, that had waded there to drink, were now hardened in the dry clay of the stream's bed ; along the banks all the willows curled up the white under-sides of their leaves, half dead for lack of rain.

The Saint, sitting up by the hermitage,

where cover was coolest, knew that this was
the merciful drought which God sends from
heaven once in a generation to the lost souls
of men. For he had read in certain holy
books how at that time all the water that
goes to and fro over the earth's surface is
sucked down by the many mouths of hell,
till even their thirst is, for the time, assuaged,
and their yoke of torture made light. Then,
that they may win ease, sorrow and affliction
are given to all that here has life ; that thus,
even for our lost brethren, we may feel pity,
and endure the cost of it ; even as Christ did
for us, though the cost to Him was the
drought and the death of Calvary. And by
the drought which He sends, and which we
bear, He teaches us that there is not only a
Communion of Saints but a Communion of
Sinners, as also He showed forth in His
Sermon on the Mount, wherein He taught
how God maketh His sun to shine on the
evil and on the good, and sendeth rain on the
just and on the unjust.

All this the Saint learned in his reading,

# The Merciful Drought

and also how God by His wisdom made the sea salt, lest that also should be drunk dry, and leave the earth a waterless wilderness with no more stores of rain ; also how all holy wells that belong to the Saints are left, at that time, to the dwellers on earth, so that in their affliction they may be turned to Him, and to the Church, which is His outstretched Hand let down to earth for all sinners.

The Saint pondered on all these things through the hot weariness of day, till night rose, covering the sky. Under the rock by his side the holy well brimmed large in the light of the moon ; and presently along the forest came the soft trampling of feet, and all the animals came out of the shadows to drink.

There were the hinds with their young, the hares and all the little burrowing people, the squirrels and the rest of the tree-folk, and all the root-grubbers : none of them was missing. They saw the Saint, sitting silver in the moonlight, and they waited, for they knew the well was holy and belonged to him.

Except in times of drought and famine none came to drink there but only those who had lips to confess their sins and to pray, because for them the water of the well had virtue.

Then the Saint made the sign of the Cross towards them. "Peace be with you!" he said; and at once all the herds and tribes of fur moved down together to the water to drink.

Right up to midnight they came, dipping their nozzles to the long draught: yet still the well brimmed large, and its water diminished not.

The Saint, watching, remembered how Christ fed the multitude, and how, at the last, more remained than had been broken at the beginning. Now the drought had reached its height; and every day, since the stream had disappeared, the animals had come to beg of the amiable hermit abatement for their thirst; and he had sent them away satisfied, and still the well held water to its brim.

When all had drunk, they stayed to see his hand lifted in blessing. "Go in peace!"

said the Saint, and all the herds moved back
into the forest.

But now, on this night, out of the solitude
when all were gone, a figure came and stayed.
And this one stretched out hands, and knelt
by the well's brink waiting.

The Saint, looking, saw that the Cross had
been removed from this man's brow, and that
the only covering he had for his nakedness
was a garment of outer darkness.  Therefore,
knowing to what place the other belonged, he
crossed only himself, being afraid, and spake
no word of greeting.

The man said, "Father, dip down thy
finger in the water, and lay it upon my
tongue, for I am consumed by a great thirst!"

The saint said, "Is it not the merciful
drought?  Go to thine own place, and get
drink!"

The other answered, "Last night when I
died I went down, and found there that the
merciful draught was over and the flow of
water stayed, and that all had tasted but had
left no drop for me.  Therefore for three

nights it is given me to return to the earth to find mercy of man."

"Doubt not," answered the saint, "that the time of thy death was in God's Hands; return, therefore, whence thou camest!" Then the doomed man and the saint arose each and went to his own bed.

The next day when the saint looked out over the forest, still the drought was not gone; and when he came to the well he found that it had run dry. "It is the lost soul," thought the saint, "whose coming has driven away the water."

When it was night all the herds came up out of the forest to drink, as they had been used to do before; by the side of the empty well the saint sat weeping. They stood watching him, and waiting for the word to be spoken.

The saint prayed, "O Lord, open the hard rock, and let Thy mercy rush forth!" But the place of the waters remained dry. And still all the animals watched and waited for the sign.

64

## The Merciful Drought

At midnight a sudden fear took hold of them, and they fled ; and there came to the well's brink once more the same form of a man, who stooped and looked in. " Last night," he said, "more water was sent to the souls ; but I got none of it, having come here to find mercy. Now, therefore, dip down thy finger, and cool my tongue ; for I am tormented with this thirst."

The saint said, " Thy coming has troubled the waters ; for they are holy, and thou art accursed, and thy presence has dried them and driven them back. Go hence, and return no more ! "

"Yet once I must return ! " answered the other ; and he rose sadly, and left that place.

All the next day the saint heard lamentations and cries of suffering through the forest ; and he knew that all the wild things were perishing for lack of the water that had failed. And now, there being no drain or drop left in the holy well, the saint himself was feeling the pains of thirst ; and all night without sleep he had heard the moans of the forest in pain, and

no succour could he bring. Thus there came
to him a sense of his own unworthiness, which
years of solitude by his well of sweet waters
had made him forget. So the next night he
knelt praying by the dried spring, that water
might come forth, not for himself, but that
the beasts of the forest might live.

And ever more and more the thirst within
him increased; and the silver moon rose in
cool pitiless strength, and struck his brain with
the fear of madness.

He grovelled and dabbled with his hands in
the yet moist mud where the well-water had
lain. "Now I feel the pains of the damned!"
he said, and knew that presently all sense and
life would be taken from him.

To and fro within the forest went the
trampling of feet, and the soft scurry of
furred creatures; but to-night none came
near him. The holy waters had failed, and
the saint had turned God's poor away empty.
All around him was solitude to the eye; he
saw the moon moving on to the hour which
must bring him death. There he bowed and

lay low on the stone brink of the well. "O God, have pity on me," he said, "for I have sinned !"

Out from under the trees paced a stag, milk-white, lifting up its head to the moon. Between its antlers it held the blessed rood, and upon every tine burned a clear taper, unbent by the wind. The saint beheld there the stag of Saint Hubert.

Slowly it moved down to the spring, still lifting its front to the light in the heavens overhead ; and all the while the saint crouched watching, frozen with holy fear. At last the stag's feet stood at the well's brink, and out of its eyes, that were raised to the moon, large tears grew and began falling apace. Softly sobbing there for the sorrow of the whole forest, and of meek creation in pain, it looked intercessor and pleader for its own kind where the help of man had failed. Then, when its tears rained no more, it turned about and went back into the gloom of the forest, and the saint was left alone.

Looking down he saw that, where the stag's

tears had fallen, a small pool of water had risen, enough for a man to hold in the hollow of his hand. The saint saw all his thirst at an end, and stooped down his lips to drink. "Blessed be God," he said, "blessed be His holy name!" And as he said so, he saw by his side the same shape as on former nights, and the lips of the doomed man opening towards him in the gloom, and the hands reaching out and pleading for thirst to be quenched.

And now the saint's suffering had made a brother of him; and he made the sign of the cross towards the man, saying, "Now I know thy sorrow: drink, and be satisfied, and depart from me in peace!"

He dipped down his hand into the well, and drew out the drops of water in the hollow of his palm for the other to drink. There was a sigh of indrawn waters, like the sound of a great river going down to the sea; and the saint's hand was hot and dry, as if it had been held to the mouth of a furnace; but the man's form was no longer there. And suddenly all the waters of the well lay large and brimming to the moon.

Then from the forest came the trampling of many feet, and all the herds and furred things, the stag of Saint Hubert leading them.

The saint made the sign of the cross toward them. "Peace," he said, with parched lips, "Peace be with you!" And slowly and solemnly all the four-footed ones moved down and drank at the stream.

There came a sound of the quenching of many thirsts, and to the saint it was as good as the sweetest Sanctus bell ever heard on earth. And when all the beasts had well drunk, and gone back into the forest, leaving the saint alone, then he, with deep humility, took his place in that lowest room which God had given him for his body's need.

And as he drank and drank, there came rain, and the patient heart of heaven was loosed.

WHAT know ye of the wounds of Christ,
  Ye friends for whom He died ?
For you at least the love sufficed,
  When Love was crucified.

For you, whose feet He plucked from hell,
  He perished not in vain :
For you, when that He died, He fell
  That He might rise again.

I watch the wounds : for me how vain
  The blood-drops from His side,
Poor God, who perished in His pain,
  Curst, spit upon, denied !

Little ye know the pangs He bore,
　　Ye friends whom Love forgave :
There was a bitterer wound He wore
　　For souls He could not save.

FROM these thy servants who behold
　　Thy face continually,
To whom 1 gave large gifts of gold—
　　Shall this my guerdon be ?

Since once I served them, wasting so
　　My substance at their board,
Have they no broken meats to throw
　　The beggar of their lord ?

Thy swine, they lack not to be fed,
　　Though I stand famished by ;
And all thy hirelings eat thy bread,
　　When I for hunger die !

71

The meats stand ready to be carved,
    The sparkling wines are spiced ;
Then, give me room, lest I be starved
    Back to the Feet of Christ !

# THE TREE OF GUILE

# THE TREE OF GUILE

HADOWS of leaves fell through the windows of the priory into the monks' cells: soft-textured leaves of the early summer with the sun in them. A green tint shed itself through the warm veins, and fell where the shadows danced on the monks' missals, between the eyes of the holy men, and the holy words.

The novices saw in them the limbs and the wings of the wood-folk, and crossing themselves for fear, drew back into the darker corner of their cells, leaving the sun to make a square of light on the stone floor for the tree-dancers to dance in.

But the Father Prior smiled, and letting his

mind go dreaming over the holy legends of
saints,—"God is good," he said to himself,
"and maketh the thoughts of all that turn to
Him pure."

Presently the bell rang at the outer gate,
and the porter, entering the Prior's cell, said :
"It is your son, father, who is come and would
speak with you."

Then the old man rose, and went in haste
to the chapel, and to the figure of our Lord
which was there : and he knelt, saying :
"Sweet Father Christ, that bell that sounded
to Thee but now, was for the coming of Thy
prodigal son, Absalom, who has been gone
from Thee now a year. Give me leave,
therefore, to bring forth the best robe and put
it on him, and a ring on his hand, and shoes
on his feet ; and let us make merry and be
glad, seeing that the young man is yet
alive !"

Then he went forth from there, and came
unto the wicket; and there looking through
saw his son, a most fair youth passing into
man's estate, and all his head was heavy with

golden hair that flowed far and wide upon his shoulders.

The Prior put his hands through the wicket, and caught hold of the lad's face on both sides, and drew it within the lintel of the door. Then he kissed him right tenderly, asking him how he did.

" I do ill, father," answered the youth.

" Nay, I know, I know !" said the Prior. "Easter is now passed, and thou didst not come to receive Christ's Body to thy poor famishing soul. Our Lord was sorrowful in His feast for this."

" Father," said the young man, " make peace with Him for me, and receive my confession ! I saw Him in the city, at the Church of the Assumption, last night ; and all through the procession, His Eyes were upon me like coals of fire. Then I knew that I had grieved thee, whom He loves, and I came to seek thy blessing ; but I would not enter till thou camest to bid me welcome."

" Enter without fear," answered the Prior; " even now He waits for thee in the chapel."

And he undid the bars, and drew his son
across the threshold. Then the Prior went
in, and sat himself down below the choir ;
and the young man came and knelt with his
face between his father's knees : " Give me
your blessing," said he, " for I have sinned ! "
The Prior said to him : " Tell all, see that
thou hide nothing ! " The young man answered : " Father, my sin is, I cannot see
God."

" Blessed are the pure in heart, for they
shall see God ! " said the Father. " Thou art
not pure."

" How can I be pure, when I am young ? "

" Christ was young," said the Prior, " yet
He was pure."

" He had a pure mother ! " answered the
youth : and the old man sighed.

After a while, seeing how his son kept
silent, he went on : " When thou art tempted
to sin, then within thy heart say : " Thou
God seest me."

" That," said the youth, " angers me ; since
*I* cannot see God. In the darkness He looks

at me with an evil Eye. If I loved Him as I
love thee, it would not hurt me : I should not
feel Him ever like a horn in my back. Nay,
father, until I love God I am certain to sin.
Thou hast learned to love God, and hast no
sin and no temptation ; yet in the past *I* was
thy sin; and now I bear all the temptation."

His father said : " Stay with me and the
brethren, this one night, while I hear what
the Lord would say concerning thee; and to-
morrow I will let thee go. Only to-night be
a little sorry for thy sins."

So that evening all the monks made merry
because the son of their Prior was come to be
their guest. They lighted a hundred candles
before the rood, in thanksgiving to the five
Wounds of Christ that bled once for all
sinners.

At midnight, when all slept, the Prior
knelt alone before the altar ; and said he :
" Sweet Father Christ, open the young man's
eyes that he may see, and visit not on him
the offences of his parents ! Nay, Jesu, Who
lovest both who were the cause of him, Who

hast given peace unto her, and hast done away my iniquity, give me now to suffer temptation in the stead of my son. I ask no better than for a year to let this be, until Easter be come; when he, being for so long a time untempted shall be made pure in heart and see God, as I also, by the ruth that Thou hast towards me, do see Him continually."

In the morning he said to his son : " Take God with thee, and go ; only promise me one thing, that until thou be tempted thou wilt commit no sin. And at Easter come again and receive thy Maker, and see if it be not well with thee ! "

So the young man gave that promise, and his father him absolution of all that had gone heretofore. Then he received his Saviour, and departed again to the city.

Presently the Prior, who had led so quiet and holy a life all these many years, became greatly moved to sin ; and for all the penances he might do never did the pain abate. Day and night his flesh strove with him, seeking to cast him out of the sight of God.

# The Tree of Guile

Daily, showing his sorrow before the Cross, he said : " Thou seest, Father Christ, how sorely Thy son has been tried in these years; and how, not knowing Thee, he must needs go astray, and how there was no help for him since he had not Thee. Nay, did I not wear Thy Cross constantly before mine eyes, and Thy grievous great wounds in my body, I could not keep from falling ! "

Every day he read continually of Christ's Charity to sinners, also of the ways of Grace for the healing of the seven deadly sins ; yet each day and night temptations of body and soul returned to him, as though in no way had he vanquished them previously.

Yet when the love of God seemed momently to fail him, the love of his son bore him in its stead ; and he would weep tenderly for the young man's past sorrows, saying : " Alas, my son Absalom, is it thus thou hast been afflicted ? "

Now all the monks wondered greatly how age and sorrow every day wrought such change in the Prior's aspect ; yet therewith the sweetness of his nature increased, so that it seemed his face shone when he spoke to them.

In the season of Lent, when spring was in the air, his trouble was so great that barely could he rise up off his knees lest sin should get the better hand of him, and throw him from grace. But at the time of our Lord's Passion he was cheered greatly, for word came to him from his son, saying that in all things he had kept to the letter of his promise, and been without sin such as he could name; and that at Easter he purposed coming to receive his Lord, if might be, there, or, if not, in some other place; trusting that after that his eyes might be opened and he might see God.

Now on the Friday before Easter, which is the day of our Lord's death, the Prior knelt before the Cross praying, because of the heavy burden of sin that was upon him for his son's sake; and cried he, stretching up his hands: "Rue on me, Jesu, for Thy five wounds, and for Thy piteous agony, endured for our sorrows!" And as he spoke he felt as it were fire striking upon his hands and side, and also upon his feet; and looking he beheld that he had received the signs of our Lord's Passion, even as our blessed Father Francis did at one time.

Then he said in himself, "Surely this is a token of my son's deliverance from sin, and that my offering is acceptable." And he blessed God exceedingly, far more for His mercy than for the miracle done in his own body. And being of an humble mind he let none of the brethren know of the honour Christ had done to him; but, when any were by, covered his hands and feet that the marks might not be seen.

So the time passed of that and the next day, till it was the night before Easter: and while he knelt watching by our Lord's tomb for the coming of the angels at dawn to roll off the stone, he was aware that his former peace of mind had returned to him, and that his burden of temptations was loosed. Howbeit not on that Easter day, nor in the week following did his son come to ring at the monastery gate.

83

## All-Fellows

Yet, in truth, the night before, the young man had come, after a long journey, within sight of the Priory : and all the year past he had been sinless for anything he could think or name, having had no temptation. And as he went he wondered at himself, for his heart was pure, yet he could not see God.

And now he was come close to the ascent which mounts up to the walls of the Priory : just there below the orchards begins a glade, leading out of the high-road, where many hawthorns and other trees are. It was the hour between late and early when night is about to cease, and dawn has not yet begun : doubtless in Rome, whence all things in Christ's Church have their source, the Easter sun had already risen.

Now as he came under that glade, the young man felt all the peace that had been there pass out of his heart ; for that was the same moment when the Prior's burden, that he had borne so long, was loosed from him, at the fulfilment of the time in which he had prayed that for his son's sake he might suffer.

# The Tree of Guile

To the left side, a little away from the track stood a tree in young green leaf, and up among the boughs sat a woman, as naked as the Devil can make her; and her flesh was all polished and smooth. Amongst the dull wood-shadows, liquid and mellow a light played round her, and the tree crackled at its roots, as though they were thrust through the earth into some underground fire to draw sustenance from thence.

That fair young Absalom, who for a year had had no temptation to try him either for good or ill, or to mix strength with his weakness, was as a bird to her lure. When he came where she sat above, she but reached down her hand and wound it in all his yellow hair, and drew him up to her into the tree. " We will make merry blossom together ! " said she, and laid her wicked body by his in the heart of the boughs.

Easter passed, and no news was brought to the Prior of his son : and again the young summer came over the earth, and threw the

dance of its leaves through the windows of
the Priory, and on to the pages of the monks'
books where they sat and read.

The Prior took a fair missal in his hand—
all its borders were coloured with fine work-
manship—and went out through the orchards
and down into the glade beyond, reading as
he went. Sorrow at the long absence of his
son made him turn ever to the wounds of
Christ, asking help of them for the absent
one. Also he read the ways by which Grace
is to heal sinners of the seven deadly sins.
Thus he went under the bright waving
branches, seeing the shadows of their leaves
pass between him and the holy words.

Presently, being weary, he sat himself
down under one tree, musing of the words he
read. Down hung long golden chains of
blossom here and there, everywhere over his
head. As he held the book open a whole
shower of them fell, covering the last page he
had read. He lifted his hand to turn to the
next meditation, and as he brushed the
blossoms by he saw that all the page was

wiped clear of writing, not a line there remained : all the holy words relating to the first of the deadly sins, and how it might be guarded against, were blotted out, and only the fair white parchment remained.

In a dream he turned to the next passage; and again the golden blossoms unchained themselves from the tree, and fell, hiding out every word : and when he swept them away, all the words were gone.

"What miracle is this that God does?" thought the Prior; and he turned again with hands that wore faint the marks of our Lord's Passion. Once more blossoms fell over the page that he had opened; and when he cast them off, the words they had covered were wiped away.

At last he turned to where the sins of pride and presumption are told of, and their danger to men's souls, and the remedy through meekness to the will of Christ. And now, trembling, the Prior cast loose the blossoms that fell, and saw that of all the words which were wiped out only a few remained as before.

There alone upon the page were to be seen these words of the scripture :

"And no man may redeem his brother, nor make agreement unto God for him ; for it cost more to redeem their souls, so that he must let that alone for ever."

And thereupon the tree crackled, as though its roots below were on fire. Truly in that moment the Prior knew that God's doing was about to be revealed to him. He lay with his head leaned back, so that his ear was to the trunk of the tree ; and within there he heard sobbing and crying, and his son's voice calling to him out of the pains of hell.

There, by compulsion of the Father of lies, it spake thus unto him : "Ah, Father, how blind thou wast in the innocence of thy heart, loving God, not knowing Him ! Wherefore didst thou take on thee my temptations and not my sins : for before I was conceived those sins, which thou didst not, were ordered to be done. So, in a single night I did them all, and passed for ever from life to the bondage of hell."

# The Tree of Guile

When the Prior heard his son's voice speak
that, with anguish of heart he believed it,
and lay for a great while as one dead. Then
he lifted himself up and cried : "Now I, that
have been pure of heart, have seen God face
to face !"

He stretched up his hands in an agony of
love, crying : "Cursed be God ; cursed be
His Holy Name !" And at that, for pure
sorrow of the words, his heart broke, and all
Christ's wounds that were upon his body fell
to bleeding.

And as he lay so bleeding to death, his
blood fell upon the tree's roots, and ran down
into the earth. Then the whole tree cracked
and was torn as if the lightnings of God had
smitten it, and all its chains of fire withered
and died and fell down, so that it was left
bare. And the tree-witch loosed from the body
the soul of the fair young Absalom whom
she had held there bound : so was that ante-
chamber to hell made void and desolate for
ever.

After a time came the Brethren, and found

their Prior lying dead, with the marks on his body of our Lord's Passion. Then they, knowing him to be a Saint, bore him up to the Priory, and buried him in the chapel under the high altar; and there, for such as loved God, were many miracles done in pity of him whose heart broke at cursing the Holy Name, and in token of the forgiveness that all love wins.

Spring comes with silent rush of leaf
　　Across the earth, and cries,
"Lo, Love is risen!"　　But doubting Grief
　　Returns, "If with mine eyes

"I may not see the wounds, nor reach
　　"My hand into His side,
"I will not hear your lips that preach
　　"Love raised and glorified.

"Unless I see the wounds that brake
　　"His heart, and marred His brow
"Most grievously for sorrow's sake,
　　"How shall I know Him now?"

91

Love came, and said, " Reach hither, Grief,
    "Thy hand into My side :
"O, slow of heart to win belief,
    "Seeing that for grief I died.

"Lo, all the griefs of which I died
    "Rise with me from the dead ! "
Then Grief drew near, and touched the side,
    And touched the wounds that bled ;

And cried, "My God, O blessed sign,
    "O Body raised, made whole,
"Now do I know that Thou art mine,
    "Upholder of my soul ! "

O, LORD of love, who holdest light,
    Hear Thou the darkened speech :
Behold the eyes that know not sight,
    The hands that vainly reach.

Thou knowest all ; Thou wilt not grieve
    If in the ways of grief
I speak amiss.   Lord, I believe,
    Help Thou mine unbelief !

Lo, as the east is from the west,
    And from the north the south,
So from the sorrow of my breast
    Are the words of my mouth.

Let but my son walk in Thy way,
    Though I be bound to hell;
And I will lift my head and say
    Thou doest all things well.

# THE KING'S EVIL

THE KING's SON

# THE KING'S EVIL

N the night which went before His death, we know how Christ gave to His disciples an example of humility, that even to this day is followed by the Kings of certain countries. This is the washing of men's feet, however lowly and poor they may be, done on Maundy Thursday, by which earthly Kings exalt themselves in striving to the pattern of their Lord's great humility.

Now, in a country where they did this, many generations ago, it had chanced that the King being an ill ruler, and false to his crown-oaths, had been driven out and supplanted by his brother who, if no better at heart than his predecessor, used his means of power more prudently. Thus it came about that, of the two brothers, one was a beggar with no friend to succour him, and the other lord of a great city, and of all the country lying for many leagues around it ; and which one hated the other most, he who was supplanted or he who had done the supplanting, it were hard to say.

On the year following this turn-over of their fortunes, it being the morning of Maundy Thursday, the new King entered the palace-courtyard like a servant, girdled with a towel, and carrying a golden ewer in his hands. There, all about the walls, sat the beggars waiting for the King's service ; and the King knelt down before each, as the custom was, and poured out water into a gold dish, and washed the feet of all.

And when he came to the last beggar of all, he found that it was his own brother, whom he hated more than aught else in the world, who had brought his feet there to be washed.

Wit ye well, the Devil was at that

christening, though not a word did the brothers speak. And the King washed right foot and left foot, and dried them with all care, as if to say, "See, you are to me even as these, mere beggars, for whom custom makes me do this thing."

Now this that happened once, happened again each year, on Maundy Thursday, at the washing of the feet : there, last of all, sat the King dethroned, and the brother who had supplanted him came and knelt, and washed his feet as he had done for all the other beggars. And to the one it was the sweetest moment of all the year, and to the other the bitterest.

To the Devil also it became a red-letter feast-day, to cheer him through the dolorous time of Easter, so great was the joy wrought for him by the hatred of the two brothers.

After some years of keeping this bitter anniversary, supplanter and supplanted disappeared from the eyes of men on one and the same day, and went the way their hearts took them. The Devil made them to be his footstool, one under his right foot and one under his left, for he would not have their hatred die for lack of remembrance.

Presently, as time went on, the Devil looked up and laughed. "Out yonder," he said, "your feast-day on earth is beginning. Come, and we will see how the little King keeps the custom that his father and uncle kept so well!"

The Devil clapped a soul into the cleft of each hoof, and went up to earth, like a diver who swims up to the surface of the deep sea.

The young King came down into the palace-courtyard, girdled with a napkin and carrying a golden ewer in his hands. His face was made holy by awe and love, because it was his first time of performing the solemn rite which had its pattern in the humility and love of Christ.

All round the walls sat the beggars with bare feet, and the Devil sat last of them : where hatred had sat all those years before, there he crouched with feet and face folded in the brown robe of a mendicant, and waited for the washing to come to his turn.

The King was little more than a child; and to him this old worn-out custom was the newest and strangest thing he had ever had to do with, more strange than the touching for "the King's evil," which was done on all feast-days. He thought of the disciples in the supper-room, on the night before the Passion; and as he went from beggar to beggar he had in mind Christ with His friends the Saints: so, in each one of the beggars, he washed as it were the feet of some Saint.

"This," he said of the first, "must be Peter!" for he was a true child of the Church, and he knew that Peter must ever come foremost. So he washed Peter's feet diligently and humbly, making mental submission to all the dogmas which from then to this had infallibly come from him. Then he passed on. "And this shall be John!" he thought, at the next, for that saint was ever the one he loved the best. Then he came to

James, and then Andrew : and so he went on till he had washed all the feet down to Thomas : then there was one left. " This must be Judas," he sighed, as he knelt down to offer water to the last.

The Devil untucked his robe, and let down his two hoofs into the gold dish. The young King drew back his breath, first in disgust, and then in pure pity, at sight of those deformed feet : and he thought of Judas, and the fiery way his feet had trodden at the last. And he thought, "To all the others I have prayed; but for this one may I pray ? "

Then he laved the right foot tenderly, and the left foot tenderly, and dried them both : and at the end " Oh, God," he said, " make these lame feet whole ! " And saying this he stooped forward and kissed them.

The Devil uttered a cry : for the two souls, which he had brought back with him out of Hell, had slipped from his hold, and had passed up into the lowest room of Purgatory.

## The King's Evil

The Devil drew up his feet painfully, and wrapped them in his robe, while with the best will in the world he let his curse go out on the mortal who had so robbed him. And the young King's lips were all blistered, as he rose up from that washing a white leper.

When the people saw what had befallen, they made sure that it was from God, a sign of His judgment on an evil house in its last generation. Therefore they made haste, and stripped the King of his royal robes, and drove him out beyond the city-walls to a leper's life among the solitary and waste places ; and in his room they appointed a magistracy to rule over them, for of the royal house no male of the direct line was left.

The leper King bore all meekly, knowing that his leprosy was but a symbol of the sins of himself and of his father's house : so putting on sackcloth he went out to live in a lonely hut far from the high-road, and not near any of the farms or tilled fields. In a path that ran hard by up to the hill-pastures, he put an earthen bowl, wherein sometimes food for him was set by the charitable, and sometimes not, as might chance. And never did any man see his face.

Only on one day in the seven must he come back to the place where before he had been King ; that was when all the bells rang, and at the great church in the city Mass was sung. Then he would cover his face over with a cloth, and hang the leper's bell about his neck, and go along byways, and by a side-gate, and through narrow streets till he was come to the Close and to the chancel's north side where the lepers' window was. There he would kneel and look in, and behold the miracle of the Mass, and hear a little of the words ; and quickly, after the third bell had been rung, turn and go while the streets were still void. And if at any time he saw a man coming his way, he would sound the bell about his neck, and cry "Unclean !" So they two would pass upon opposite sides, or else the other would turn, not to meet him, and draw away into a side-street till he had passed by. After a time he became used to that grief and shame ; and to go and hear Mass was the one joy he had with God and his fellow-man.

Now it happened, one day of High Mass, that, as he was going along a poor narrow street, there was a child playing upon one of the steep flights of steps that lead up to the doors; and as the leper passed the child slipt, and cried, feeling itself falling. Then, forgetting that no help might come from him, the King put out his hand and caught the little one, and set it upon its feet. Its mother within the house, hearing the cry, ran to the door, and saw a leper handling her own flesh and blood. At that sight, between fear and rage, she threw at him the thing that first came, then seizing up a mop-stick made out after him, dealing him many hard knocks with it, and at last casting it after him as a thing that had become unclean for further handling. The leper bowed down his head and went on, stricken to the heart that not for the love of God might he do kind deed to any of his fellow-creatures.

# All-Fellows

The mother picking up her child carried it in, to wash it clean from any taint of leprosy : but when she was stripping it with shrill scoldings, all at once her voice stopped at mid-word, as her eyes fell on its bared flesh; for there, where before the child had borne the marks of the 'King's evil,' the skin was now whole and sound.

The next time the leper went by, a week after, a woman came carrying a child and following him : and she was a sister of the other woman whose child he had caught in its fall. When there was no one else in the street but themselves, she came close : "Touch my child !" she whispered ; and at that the leper moved more quickly, ringing his bell to warn her off. "I am unclean !" he said. The other did not cease following, but whenever others came in sight she drew back, as if fearful lest she should be seen ; then, as soon as they two were alone again, she came, saying, "For the love of God, touch my child !"

For the love of God! The leper turned his

eyes and looked. Through the cloth over his face he saw the mother uncovering the child's throat ; and there upon it was the mark of the King's evil. "For the love of God, Oh, for the love of God !" she wept.

The leper stood still ; he reached out his hand trembling, and made the sign of the Cross over the scars. Then he turned and ran : nor did he hear the mother's cry of thankfulness, as she blessed God to behold the healing that his touch had brought.

That day he went back out of the city by another way; and always afterwards he crept in by a different gate, and by other streets, till he reached the lepers' window within the chancel's north side. But one day as he knelt looking in at the priest saying Mass, he heard footsteps behind, and saw three women coming to where he was ; and one was carrying a child in her arms, and one was leading another woman by the hand. When they were near to him the two women stood still, and said, " For the love of God make these whole !"

"This is my only child," said one. "This is my sister," said the other; "she is a deaf-mute, the King's evil has been upon her ever since she was born."

"I am unclean!" said the leper.

"God knows," said the mother, "if you can heal my little one, you are not unclean in His sight."

The King looked in through the lepers' window, and saw the priest about to lift up the Host; and with the three women he bowed himself to the ground at the consecration. Then the leper looked toward the Body of Christ and prayed, "O, Love of God, come by way of the lepers' window and give healing to these!" Then he made the sign of the Cross upon each, and turned and went swiftly away.

Presently through all the city the whisper went by stealth how the leper's touch had healing in it, as if he were still King by divine right, and had power such as in old time was given to good kings to do good to God's poor on earth. So, in a while, the sound of

# The King's Evil

his bell, which was to warn men as he entered any street, served as a summons to those who had need of him to touch them for the King's evil. Yet still, as he went through the poor crowds that blessed him, the leper-king wore the cloth over his face, and cried "Unclean !"

At first the tale of it had been slow, for there had been doubt and fear that a leper, cut off from all men by the Finger of God, should do this thing : but presently, when the secret had passed through more than three hands, the city grew loud with it. And the cry of the poorer people was, "Give us back our King ! for God, though He curses him in his own body, blesses him in all on whom he lays hands." But for a time the priests and magistrates could not hear of such a thing as for a leper to be upon the throne.

Nevertheless the healing was apparent, for many known cases had been cured ; and at last the popular cry could no longer be withstood. For each Sunday, before and after Mass, the whole city was in a tumult, as the leper-king came and went, with his face covered, and his bell ringing about his neck.

At last seeing that his coming made strife and uproar on God's day, the leper remained in his own hut, in the fields beyond the walls, and listened for the great bell to be rung at the elevation of the Host.

But when it was found that he meant not to come, but would stay in meekness apart from God's altar, then as one man the city rose up, and went and brought him back in triumph, and put on him again the royal robe, and set him upon the throne. And, the thing being done, no voice small or great was lifted against it.

But the King was a leper still ; and still, for all man might say, beneath his crown he wore the cloth over his face, and round his neck the bell to warn men of his coming.

And as he went through the palace where all bowed down at his approach, he still cried, "Unclean, unclean !" nor would he allow any to touch him save it were for the cure of the King's evil, a thing that he thought to be a special mercy which, in his sins, God had given him. And when he went forth to Mass with a great train, and in all his royal robes, through the streets, at the church-door, he and the rest parted : and they went within, but the King passed round to the lepers' window on the chancel's north side, and there-through he heard Mass said. And from touch of him no harm came to any man ; though a leper he remained, more loved by all than any king of sound body had been in the world before.

So time went on, and it was Maundy Thursday once more. Into the courtyard came the leper-king, girdled with a towel, and bearing the golden ewer ; and there all round the walls sat the beggar-men waiting for their feet to be washed.

The leper over his face was wearing the cloth, and as he moved, the bell that was round his neck rang ; and he went from one to another thanking God for having put it into his hands to do that solemn service, which he had never hoped could be his to do

more. So going the round in meek thanksgiving he came to the last.

That one, at the King's coming, drew up
His beggar's rags, and set down Feet marred
and maimed into the golden dish. The
leper, when he saw that, drew in his breath
sharp, and trembled with exceedingness of
joy ; but nothing was said there. Only after
the washing he stooped low, and kissed the
two Wounds : and still could say no word
for the bliss and comfort that had there taken
hold of both body and soul. And therefrom
never again could he draw his lips away, for
in Them mercy and truth were met together,
and righteousness and peace kissed each
other.

His people, seeing how the King lay low
before a beggar's feet, thought he had fallen
from some sickness ; and going to lift him,
first saw they his hands all pure of the
leprosy. Then in wonder they drew the
face-cloth from his face, and behold, there
too all the leprosy was gone. And the bell,
as they lifted him, that was about his neck,

made no sound as it swung, to tell men that anything unclean was in their midst : but in all ways he was the most beautiful King that ever men swathed for burial

Within the church, and within the chancel's north side they buried him : where the Wound was in Christ's Side, there in the church they buried him : within the lepers' window, in between that and the high altar.

There until now the King's body, which was corrupt in life, stays incorruptible for the final day, when Christ shall at last appear, and lay His Finger upon all the world, and heal it of the King's evil.

You hear a blind man preach the light
    Wherein he never dwelt,
Because his hands can handle right
    The darkness that is felt.

O, Face of Love, to which I kneel,
    What likeness lies between
This touch of hands outstretched to heal,
    These lips that cry " unclean ! "

But when these hands have hold on fire,
    And these lips fire for breath,
And life goes down to its desire
    In the red pit of death :

Then, clear of sight in that far place,
  I may lift eyes above,
And see you looking in God's Face,
  O face I used to love !


WHEN we are parting face from face,
  Each to our destined end,
I know that God shall find no trace
  In you of me, your friend.


There where I trod the way was wide,
  With room enough for two ;
And yet I put you from my side,
  That God might look on you.


And I have bowed Him from His height
  To take this gift of me,
That pure and holy for His sight
  I left you utterly.

For single as the Heart of God,
  My heart, that loved you well,
Died for you all the while I trod
The downward path to hell.

# WHEN PAN WAS DEAD

# WHEN PAN WAS DEAD

N the woods that muffled the convent's walls Spring was letting herself show. Wherever the search went life was to be found pushing life through the moist soil, or thrusting green horns through last year's bark of trees. A gentle desire of life, half infantile, half marital, was beginning to be abroad; and nature felt the suckling's becoming the wooer's request.

The woodling looked out, blinking the long winter-sleep from her eyes: all the fibres and dead leaves and ferns, in which she had wrapped herself chrysalis-wise, she peeled off, and, lying down, rolled her clear brown skin over the newly carpeted earth.

# All-Fellows

She went up like a squirrel into a tree, and, perching from bough to bough, searched in the clefts and crannies for food.

The chatterers cried as she went, "Here is the woodling, she is after our nuts!" They pelted her with hard cones and husks that were not good to eat. She laughed mimicingly, and gave chase, till at length, tiring of the frolic, she swung herself to earth, and made through the thick underwood toward a noise of waters running in the hollow below.

All day she made the round of her haunts, searching for her own kind : but now she was the only woodling left of the tribes there had used to be. For here and there she chanced upon a sight that made her turn quickly away—of something lying quiet in a cleft of ground, or under a hollow of roots, like a large brown chrysalis without any sign of life : and she knew that whatever had not stirred then, from its winter-sleep, would stir in the world no more.

For all those wood-mates of hers she had a vague love : she could not remember one from other, and yet they had all been dear. And now she felt a new hunger for companionship rise in her heart ; and her love of those who had turned to root became cruel and sad.

Deep twilight shadows gathered up the slopes of the wood : soon the birds and squirrels went in to sleep, leaving her lonely. She stood still, stretching out her two arms, and sighed.

Down from the heights where the convent was, came the sound of the Angelus-bell, giving its domestic tinkle to the small sisterhood of nuns. Up there, pale lights shone from the chapel and the barred windows of the cells. Therein went the life of comradeship : but the little woodling was all alone. The woods pressed up to the very walls, and shadowed every window with a fondling of boughs : under their shelter the woodling crept near while the twilight drew in, and stopped to listen and look.

From within came the clatter of a pail, and the sound of washing over stone floors. Presently the lay-sister appeared at the door to empty away the water; the woodling from behind her tree could have reached out an arm and touched her. The lay-sister lifted a long breath, and sighed it out again. "Oh, me!" she said, "oh, poor sad me!" and she picked three little blades of young grass, and laid them to her lips. "When will these be growing over me?" she murmured, letting them fall for pure listlessness and grief. Then she went in and barred up the door; and the other remained alone.

"Why is she so sad, when she has with her so many of her own kind?" thought the woodling. "Now I am sad, having none."

She lingered without the walls, hearing the sounds of life inside: presently meal and prayer were over, and all was the silence of rest. Then from the window of the little cell guarding the door came a voice. "Oh, me! Oh, weary me!" and a sound of tears. It was the lay-sister crying herself to sleep.

The woodling climbed a long bough, and looked in: all was dark, she could see

nothing : there was sobbing. "Oh, me !
Oh, weary me !" came a sigh out of the
darkness. The woodling slipt her small thin
body between the bars, and crept into the
cell : and then, all at once, her heart sank
very low as for the first time she left free
wood and sky, and, entering an abode built
by man born to sorrow, felt the shades of his
prison-house fall upon her.

Uncomprehending compassion took hold
of her : "Sister," she said, "do you know
me ? I am from the wood : I heard you
crying, so I came."

In the darkness and half asleep, the lay-
sister said nothing ; only she heard a sweet
voice, and presently felt the soft arms and
warm breath of one sharing her hard couch.
"Are you the woodman's daughter ? " she
murmured. " Yes," answered the woodling :
but they did not mean the same thing : and
the lay-sister, thinking she had by her side
only a woodman's daughter who had strayed
late, thought no more, but dropped into a
weary slumber.

All that night she slept without waking,
but never did she wake again to be as
before : for all night the blood of the
woodling had tingled against her side, and
warmed her in her sleep, and put colour into
her pale dreams.

When she woke the woodman's daughter
was gone ; only in the place where she had
lain were a few buds of the wild yellow crocus.

The woodling, watching from her form in
the undergrowth, saw the lay-sister open the
convent doors and windows, and let in the
sun. The sunlit woods made her gaze and
gaze : she could not go on with her work.

"I have given her the wood-dream !" said
the tree-born to herself : "Soon I shall have
a companion, and shall not be lonely any
more."

At night, after all was still, she crept in
again to the lay-sister's cell ; and finding her
fast asleep, lay down by her side and let her
dream. Again she was up and gone, before
the other awoke.

The lay-sister went to and fro all day

in a dream ; first it was the voice of the woods, the sunlight, and the air, that called to her ; but beyond, and more than these, she heard life—kind human voices, and the laughter of children, and the hum of the housewife's wheel : because the wood-dream had taught her the joy of living ; and all that the little woodling wished for was but a half-way house left far behind.

So, the third night when the woodling climbed in through the window, she found no one on the bed, but only a heap of nun's garments lying, and the lay-sister gone. Though she went out and searched through the wood no comrade was waiting for her there : the one she had thought to win was gone far out to the ways of men : the little woodling had taught her too much.

She went back into the cell, where as in a tomb the white garments were lying folded, and wept, for she was companionless. Then she thought, " Since she has gone away there is room here for me. I will be in her place, and will teach them to be happy ! "

## All-Fellows

She put on the habit, and at dawn opened the convent doors. She knew that the lay-sister was the only one who went and came, and that all the other nuns were close prisoners, never to go forth at all. Now she went curiously from place to place : much of the life she had already learned from looking in through the wood-bowered windows : but the tiny chapel through its windows of thick glass she had never seen.

When she entered she heard from behind the grill by the altar the thin, gnat-like wail of the nuns at their early prayers : a monotonous note of feeble pain, as though all were shut in and were trying to get out, but could not.

"I will teach them how to be happy!" said the little woodling.

There she saw by the altar the Figure of Pain : and first she believed it truly to be a man, suffering in agony. She ran to pull off the thorns, and draw out the nails, but could not, and found at last that what she handled was not truth but deceit. She saw before it, offerings of flowers and candles, and her heart sank very low. "Why," she asked, "why do they love *pain?* Ah, I will teach them to be happy!"

The nuns, whose Rule made them always keep their eyes on the ground, never saw that their lay-sister was not the same. She went and came, bringing food for the convent, and carrying up water from the stream. When the days grew longer and the spring-woods brighter,—"Soon," she thought, "I will make them come out with me into the woods." She brought roots of sweet relish that only she knew how to find, and added to the convent's meals ; and at night, when all were asleep, she crept from cell to cell, and gave them the wood-dream that should make them happy. Presently she looked for laughter; and behold, tears !

A terrible restlessness and grief seemed to weigh upon all the nuns : all day long they prayed, and beat their little breasts, and sighed.

But the woodling day by day, hoping to make her work complete, brought more and

more of the wood-life within the sacred walls.
Up between the stone flags of the chapel and
the passages where her feet passed came blue-
bells of slender colour in the shade ; creepers
trailed and climbed the walls, and the whole
inner place was sweet and fragrant with things
that grew.

"Soon," thought the woodman's daughter,
" my sisters will learn where their hearts mean
them to be ! "

Alas, for their hearts ! The sweetness of
life was causing them to break. One day the
gentle Abbess called all the nuns together,
and said : "Sisters, I cannot fail to know
how much grief and suffering is upon you all ;
on me also it falls. Our hearts are weighed
down under a sweet and heavy temptation.
Doubt not, it is for our sins we suffer thus—
living too easily, and pampering too much
the bodies God has given us to despise.
Therefore by all, I make order, that penance
and hard discipline are to be used, till we feel
our hearts made whole in us again, and our
prayers a pleasant savour to God."

# When Pan was Dead

The little lay-sister could not know what this meant, but presently she heard.

"Oh !" she wept, as the sounds came out of the cells, "how hard it is to teach mortals to be happy against their will, while they worship Pain !" She shuddered, as if her own flesh felt the scourgings which the poor nuns were putting upon their bodies. Then she waited no more, but ran down into the wood where the mandrakes grew.

"They will cry," she moaned ; "ah, how they will cry ! But my poor sisters must be made happy ; I must do it !" One by one she caught them, and drew them out of the ground ; and the mandrakes groaned and shrieked, as their roots came to the light of day.

The woodling ran back to the convent, and made haste to prepare the evening meal. All the nuns came in worn with pain ; but a little peace had found its way into their faces. They ate the dry bread and the bitter roots that the lay-sister set before them ; and then they went to their cells and lay down to sleep.

The woodling laughed, and threw off her habit, and stood up in only her brown woodland skin, and long flowing hair. The air of the early summer night was soft, and she opened wide the convent door to the light of the moon.

Presently, for the root of mandrake had done its work, one of the cell-doors slid open, and one fair nun ran out naked and silvery into the moonlight.

Another, and another; the little lay-sister counted twelve; they were all away, following the wood-dream and the mandrake's cry; and the convent was deserted.

The woodling clapped her hands and ran out. "I have peopled my woods again!" she laughed; and saw from tree to tree the gleam of their nymph-like bodies go by.

Soon the woods rang with beautiful mænad laughter; and the stream had bathers under its banks. The fair sisterhood knew nothing of themselves; only, because of the mandrake, their blood worked in them to madness; and they danced, and laughed, and sang, throwing up their arms to the moon. The thin brown woodling leapt in and out of their midst, kissing them all. She said in her cruel, kind little heart, "Have I not made them happy now?"

It grew near to the hour of dawn, as all together they came to where, in a hollow between two hills, the ground was clear of trees. From slope to slope a long swathe of mist lay hiding the ground below; overhead the light came shyly through soft unfastenings of the dusk; very slowly the air paled, unclothing a mute world.

Over the valley the white mist spread a floor at their feet. Down below there went a faint tinkling sound; the sisters looked from one to the other, trying to remember where and why they had ever heard a bell before. Soon, up through the mist, like swimmers in a sea, came the pale fronts of a flock of sheep, and the head of a shepherd driving them.

He saw, standing above cloud, twelve pale women, who whitened from head to foot as they gazed at him, and one brown. The

131

brown one laughed, and sprang like a squirrel
to a tree; but the white ones lifted their
arms with a lamentable cry, and then, like
driven deer, broke and scattered back under
cover of the wood. For the dawn had come,
and the mandrake poison had finished its
work, leaving only shame and horror.

When the shepherd had gone by, the
woodling came down from her tree and began
searching for her fellows: but even she,
searching by all the wood-ways, found none,
—so deep in had they hidden themselves with
their grief. Weeping she turned, and went
back to the convent, that stood lonely with
wide doors. "Never can I teach them to be
happy," she said, "for they love Pain!"

Then she went into the chapel, and rang
loud the bell of the early Angelus. One by
one, as the familiar sound reached their ears,
they remembered where and why they had
heard the bell before, and they crept back
again by stealth into the home that was their
own. And there they put on once more the
habit they had thrown by in one midsummer

night's madness, when the spirit of the woods was in their blood. And when they came, sad and shamed, to the refectory at the call of meal, there indeed they found bread and water all laid for them, for every one in her right place ; but their little lay-sister was gone.

She went down to the mandrake bed, and dropped her face into the torn soil. "These were my sisters," she said, "my dead sisters, my wood-sisters, whose rooted hearts I made bleed ! "

So she lay and moaned, watering the earth with her tears.

All the mandrakes that were left were awake, and they heard her. "Come down!" they called from below, "come down, sister, to our soft bed ! For here we do not know what goes on on the earth in the eye of day : only we cry if we are brought back to the light. Come down, and do not cry ! "

So, after a while the woodling was drawn down by the weight of her own tears into the

ground, and became a mandrake-root, as
these her sisters were. There she sleeps to
this day ; but if any one came and drew up
that mandrake, all the convent up on the hill
would hear it cry.

You, the dear trouble of my days,
    When life shall let me cease,
Turn once aside from kinder ways
    And look upon my peace !

Let your feet rest upon my roof,
    And for the love we bore,
Forgive the heart, so far aloof,
    You cannot trouble more.

For, if the dead man had his will,
    I doubt not he would rise,
And waste his soul in sorrow still
    With looking on your eyes.

So come, when you have lost your power,
    And pardon my release :
And set your feet to rest an hour,
    A seal upon my peace.

FAIR eyes, that never did offend
    Love that for you grew blind,
Say, have you found in me the friend
    That you had need to find ?

Or have I failed, who day by day
    Forbore to reach my end,
Because of looks that seemed to say—
    "Stay with me; be my friend!"

And I, to meet your lesser need,
    Gave mine—a dear exchange !
Now, if you saw my eyes indeed,
    How you would find them strange !

Dear love, try still to be content,
  Long since for you I died ;
And still to cheer your heart there went
  A stranger at your side.

Now, wish me well, and pass me by !
  Soon shall my rest be deep,
When full upon my eyes shall lie
  The desert sands of sleep.

Two masks my fate reserves for me,
  Whichever way I fare :
Then, must the easier mask not be
  The better one to wear ?

For here indeed the mask fits well ;
  But oh, the weary pact !
How I must mouth, and strut, and swell,
  To while away the act !

137

But then, the ease to bitter breath
    The stay to wordy strife,
When I put on the mask of death,
    And drop the mask of life !

And death will lay an easier grace
    Than life around my head :
You will not understand my face
    The better when I'm dead.

Printed by BALLANTYNE, HANSON & Co.
London & Edinburgh

# A Farm in Fairyland

" We have seldom read stories which have afforded us more pleasure than the first five of this book. They are written with strong poetical feeling, and show much lively fancy—or we might say imagination—and a warm love of birds, beasts, and flowers. Besides this they are original. We do not like the rest of the stories so much, but the five good ones are possessions in themselves."

*Athenæum.*

" ' A Farm in Fairyland' does not specially tempt us, and the fantastic engravings are somewhat grim."—*Times.*

" The first thing that strikes one is the gaunt figure of a mediæval ploughman, apparently about sixteen feet high, upon the sage-green cover. This is merely one of the passing eccentricities of the hour. The book itself is not at all of a revolutionary character, presenting as it does merely some mild little fairy tales, told in studiously simple language."—*Daily News.*

" Numerous collections of original fairy stories have made their appearance of late years, and not a few have merited the epithets of graceful and charming. ' A Farm in Fairyland," by Laurence Housman, is, nevertheless, divided from the best of them, so far as is known to us, by a gulf which we cannot denote better than by describing the author's place as on the right side of the boundary of

I

genius. While positively thrilling by the originality of his concep-
tions, he charms by their simplicity. On a small scale he endures as
well as any great master that supreme test of inventive excellence, the
reader's half-angry question, " Why did I not think of this myself ? "
Take for instance that masterpiece of pathos, the story of the one
waking man in the Sleeping Palace. The *dénouement* comes with a
shock of surprise, and yet, when this has abated, it is seen to be
perfectly natural, and, indeed, inevitable from the first. In two
other beautiful stories, which bear a strong family likeness, " The
Wooing of the Maze" and " The Rooted Lover," the working out
is equally ingenious and equally logical ; with the advantage of
being as winning in its playfulness as the other is tragic in its
pitifulness. We must not omit a word of acknowledgment of the
weird fancy of " The Shadow-Weavers," and the mystic glamour of
"Japonel," where the very soul of Teutonic witch-lore seems
concentrated in the magic pool. Nor, although Mr. Housman's
poetry will be most fully appreciated by adults, are they at all
beyond the range of children, whom his fancy and humour will
especially delight. Those acquainted with Mr. Housman's previous
achievements as an artist will not need to be told that his illustrations
to his own book are full of imagination."

Dr. Richard Garnett, in the *Sketch*.

" The stories contained in ' A Farm in Fairyland,' the meaning
of which title, by-the-by, we entirely fail to understand, are very
unequal. Two or three are charming—for instance, ' Rocking-
horse Land' and 'Gammelyn the Dressmaker.' On the other
hand, ' The Man Who Killed the Cuckoo' verges on the disagree-
able, and in ' Ke-noonie in the Sleeping Palace' the name alone is
original, the story being a sort of parody of Rip Van Winkle. But,
on the whole, the collection is above the average of modern fairy
stories."—*Guardian*.

" The illustrations are distinguished by much originality and
inventiveness in design. Sometimes the effect is very charming, as

2

in the title-page and frontispiece, but sometimes Mr. Housman's originality expresses itself in eccentricity rather than beauty."

*Speaker.*

" Full of dainty conceits, provided young readers are not frightened away by the eccentric illustrations."—*Graphic.*

" The illustrations are weird, imaginative, and full of talent."

*Manchester Guardian.*

" The illustrations are confused, and not very attractive ; but we have no doubt that any child who gets these stories for a Christmas present will derive a good deal of enjoyment from them."

*Pall Mall Gazette.*

" There are some books—singularly few—which as they fall into a critic's hands, so delight him that his appreciation is in danger of becoming a mere rhapsody.  This is one ; and the present writer, wearied of reading the new books of the season, was deploring the lack of invention or power they evinced, when he lighted upon it, and straightway forgot everything else as he read it cover to cover. Mr. Laurence Housman's work as a designer he had followed for some time, so that the delightful drawings here were not unexpected, although far beyond any previous attempts.  As an author he meets him here for the second time only ; but yet the book has at once become one of the few that he would not readily forget. . . . If you care for delicious fantasies in prose, or in picture, get this little book."—*Studio.*

# The House of Joy

" Mr. L. Housman writes well, and has a good deal of fancy.
Sometimes, indeed, he has almost too much, for it carries him and
his stories into shadowy regions, whither it is difficult for plain
readers and plain reviewers to follow him. The story we like best
is 'The Traveller's Shoes,' which deals most with common earth,
and might almost be mistaken for a genuine folk-tale told in rather
a modern method. Mr. Housman himself seems to be responsible
for the illustrations. They are far from being good."—*Athenæum*.

"Since the publication of 'The House of Pomegranates,'
nothing so worthy has been done in the domain of modern fairy tale
as Mr. Laurence Housman's 'House of Joy.' It contains eight
stories illustrated by the author. The pictures are distinguished by
that archaic sentiment and that wonderful beauty of line which are
already associated with the name of Laurence Housman. Among
the tales several are admirable, and one is a gem. 'The Story of
the Herons' and 'The White King' are as good as Andersen at
his best, coloured with a curiously modern tinge. Even in the
most melancholy of Andersen's tales the lightness of his heart shines
through, but one never feels that Laurence Housman's heart is
light. His style, fastidious and graceful though it is, lacks the
magic of the Scandinavian, the silver tone which even a translation
has failed to obscure. This is, of course, to compare Mr. Laurence
Housman with the greatest master of his art, and the 'House of
Joy' justifies us of the comparison."—*Saturday Review*.

4

"When the time comes for writing the history of Victorian literature and art a chapter or two will have to be devoted to the revival of the Fairy Tale and to the resuscitation of the art and craft of book illustration. Under both these heads the name of Mr. Laurence Housman will find an honourable place. In his 'Farm in Fairyland' he showed us that he could write fairy stories better than most contemporary authors; but in his new book, 'The House of Joy,' he displays a marked and striking improvement both in power of imagination and in excellence of style. The stories have originality, fantasy, and beauty; the illustrations are unique. The book would make a delightful present for delightful children; but on commonplace and unimaginative children it would be thrown away.'—*New Age*.

"A marvellous production. I have never seen any black-and-white work by Mr. Housman which satisfied me so much as the pictures to the 'House of Joy.' The harshness, amounting almost to crudity, of some of his earlier designs has vanished. The eager imaginative quality remains; I instance the designs for 'The Prince with Nine Sorrows,' 'The Luck of the Roses,' and 'Happy Returns' as reaching the high water-mark of imaginative black-and-white work in our time."—*Speaker*.

" The stories are pretty and original, as, for instance, ' The Prince with the Nine Sorrows'; but the gem of a good collection is, perhaps, 'The Luck of the Roses.' If the binding of the book is worthy of praise, the illustrations are, as a rule, unsatisfactory."
*Morning Post*.

"One of the prettiest of Christmas volumes. Type and paper, illustrations and text, are alike attractive."—*Guardian*.

" Exquisitely wrought and exquisitely illustrated. The writing and the drawing are alike imbued with imagination and distinction."
*Black and White*.

" Among the most original and most charming fairy tales of the

5

season. Mr. Housman writes as well as he designs. He is a born story-teller. His fairy romances are not only quite new, but they flow from his pen as naturally as if he were telling them to children. . . . Ideal fairy tales, beautiful in feeling, simple in expression, and neither too vague nor too ingenious in plot. We do not know any living writer whose stories are more certain to please children, although these will give unbounded satisfaction to their elders as well. The merits of Mr. Housman's designs are better known. Though peculiar, they are not eccentric. The flowing lines of Mr. Housman's compositions and their richness of tone distinguish them clearly from the work of any other draughtsman, and at the same time make them beautiful in spite of minor faults. . . . The heads of his figures, for instance, are now and then preposterously small."

*Manchester Guardian.*

www.ingramcontent.com/pod-product-compliance
Lightning Source LLC
Chambersburg PA
CBHW020010030726
47500CB00002B/524